ERIC
The Colorful Cricket
starts KINDERGARTEN

Dedication

To my wonderful family,

This book exists because of your unwavering belief in me. Your endless support and patience have been my anchor throughout this journey. Thank you for always standing by me.

To all the little dreamers,

This book is a reflection of my faith in you. Keep moving forward, trust in yourself, and never give up—your dreams are within reach when you follow your heart.

Masterful Person Company Publishing

www.mpcpublishing.com

©2024 Tammy Christian.

ISBN: 978-1-962771-13-9

Library of Congress Control Number: 2024919928

This is a work of fiction. All rights reserved.

ERIC
The Colorful Cricket
starts KINDERGARTEN

Tammy Christian

Illustrated by Jiya Daim

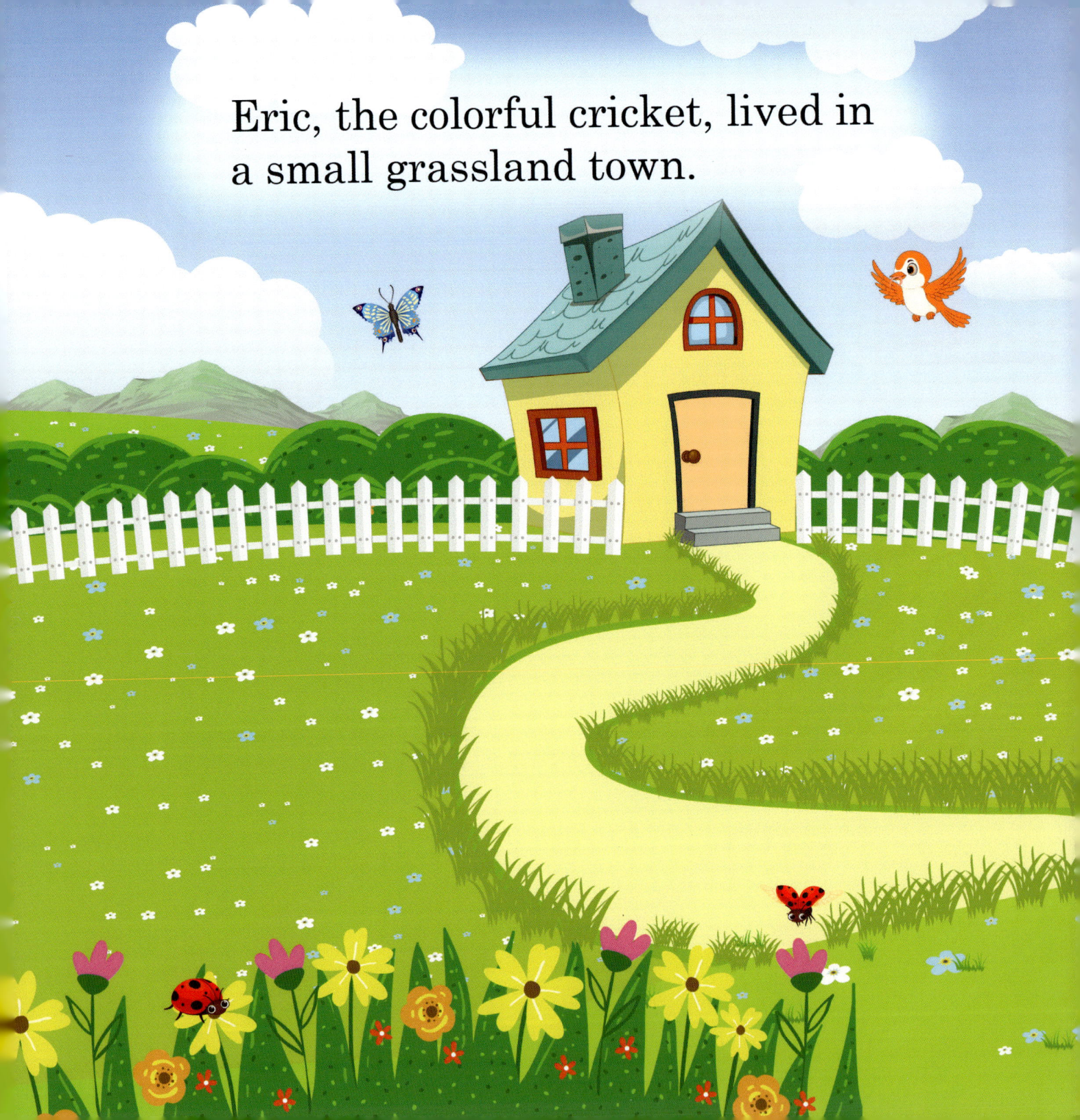
Eric, the colorful cricket, lived in a small grassland town.

He spent his summers jumping, running, and going on picnics with his family.

The sunny summer days got shorter, and Eric knew something exciting was about to begin—kindergarten!

Eric was worried about kindergarten. He wondered if the other kids would like him.

The big day finally arrived. Eric did not want to eat his breakfast.

His little sister, Pepper, noticed Eric's reluctance. "Are you feeling okay, Eric?"

"My tummy feels tickly." Eric rubbed his wings together and chirped. Eric looked at his mom with big cricket eyes. "Do I have to go to school?"

"Yes, my little one. You'll make new friends. You'll play, learn, and go on exciting adventures!"

"Eric, you're likable just the way you are. Feeling scared about new things is okay. I get scared sometimes, too, but trying new things can be exciting!"

Eric bravely puffed up his colorful wings. "Okay, Mommy, I'll try kindergarten. Maybe it'll be fun!"

Welcome to Kindergarten!

Eric arrived at school. His tummy tickled as he stood in front of his classroom door. He puffed his colorful wings and went in.

Eric made a new friend right away! They played together during recess.

Eric's teacher displayed his drawing on the classroom storyboard. A proud smile spread across his cricket face.

When the school day ended, Eric waved goodbye to his new friend.

On his way home, Eric felt happy and excited about what tomorrow would bring.

That night, after Eric was tucked into bed, he remembered the wonderful moments of his first day of kindergarten.

He was ready to explore, learn, and embark on new, exciting adventures. His tummy tickled, but this time with excitement.

Fun Facts About Why Crickets Chirp

Crickets Can Tell the Temperature.

They chirp faster when it's warm!

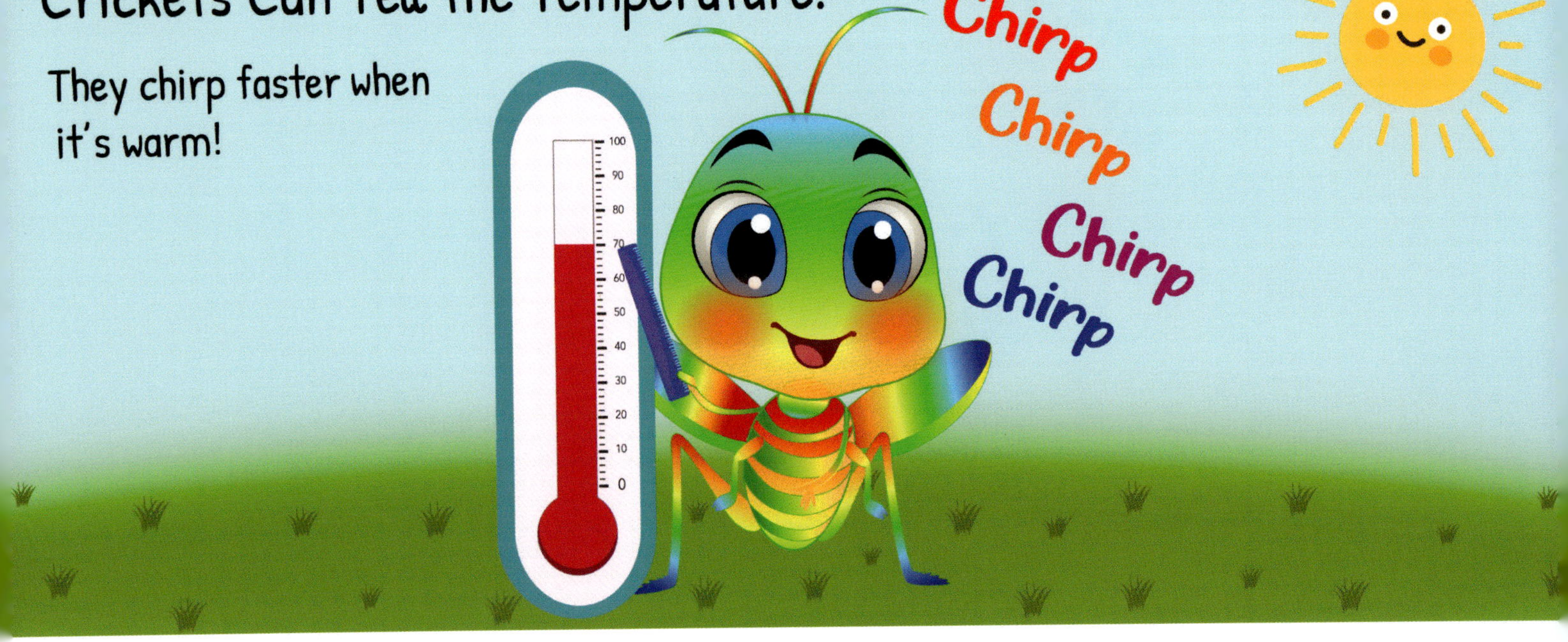

Chirp Chirp Chirp Chirp

Crickets chirp to talk to other crickets!

Chirp

HELLO!

Chirp

Crickets chirp to sing their special song! Each cricket has its own chirping rhythm, kind of like singing a little song. It's how they make themselves heard!

Chirp

Chirp
Chirp

Crickets love the night time. They chirp when it's calm and quiet.

The End.

ABOUT THE AUTHOR

Tammy Christian fell in love with storytelling as a child, spending hours creating and enjoying fun, imaginative adventures. Today, she shares that love through her career as a children's book author. In her stories, Tammy encourages kids to be brave, believe in themselves, and face challenges with confidence.

Her books feature lovable characters and positive messages that help teach important life lessons. Through stories about courage, friendship, and never giving up, Tammy reminds young readers that no dream is too big and that they can achieve anything if they follow their hearts.

Find out more at tammycauthor.com

ABOUT THE ILLUSTRATOR

Jiya Daim is an illustrator who finds magic in bringing imaginary characters to life. She creates colorful drawings that make kids want to read more. She enjoys crafting, painting, badminton, and supporting her family.

Follow Jiya on IG @childrenbooksillustrator